The Cloud Horse

& Other Stories

The Cloud Horse

& Other Stories

Strawberry Shakespeare

Diamond Star Press
LOS ANGELES

The Cloud Horse & Other Stories
Revised and Updated Edition

ISBN-10: 1475040970
ISBN-13: 978-1475040975

This book is a work of fiction. Any references to historical events, real people, or real locales are used fictitiously. Other names, characters, places, and incidents are the product of the author's imagination and any resemblance to actual events or locales, or persons living or dead is entirely coincidental.

Published by Diamond Star Press

For C. J. Dennis

(1876-1938)

Books by
Strawberry Shakespeare

NOVELS

Saving Bluestone Belle

Hope's Horse: The Mystery of Shadow Ridge

SHORT STORY COLLECTIONS

The Cloud Horse & Other Stories

NON-FICTION

The Reading Advantage: Quick & Easy Ways to Transform Your Child into a Passionate Reader!

Table of Contents

Publisher's Foreword

Welcome to this collection of extraordinary horse stories for children. We are delighted to bring you this special new edition containing the treasured classic, "The Cloud Horse," along with three original tales by bestselling author Strawberry Shakespeare—the Native American-themed "White Fire," the heartwarming horse story, "The Appaloosa Colt" and, exclusively for this new edition, a charming sequel to that story, "The Horse Whisperer Academy." We have also added a bonus selection from ***Saving Bluestone Belle,*** Strawberry Shakespeare's bestselling comic-adventure novel for young readers.

The Cloud Horse

Boys and girls who love horses and adventure will adore this exhilarating yarn about a kid who is whisked away on the back of a flying horse! This story is based on "The Boy Who Rode into the Sunset," a classic tale by C. J. Dennis and a personal favorite of children's author Strawberry Shakespeare. In her quest to bring it to modern audiences, she has made several valuable enhancements to the original which render this magical fable more meaningful and enjoyable than ever:

- The original story has been adapted as a novelette with eight exciting chapters that highlight each special part of the tale, ensuring that young readers will eagerly read on to find out what happens next.
- A beautiful cover has been specially designed for this edition. It contains an evocative image of the white horse featured in the story, which is sure to stimulate your child's imagination and thrill horse lovers of all ages.

- This new version of the story has been colorfully renamed and the chapters given intriguing titles to entice the horse kids among us!
- To enrich you and your child's reading experience, Strawberry Shakespeare explores the life and times of author C. J. Dennis in the chapter, "Who Was C. J. Dennis?"

Three Stories by Strawberry Shakespeare

Bestselling children's book author, Strawberry Shakespeare, enchants readers of all ages with the mystical and inspiring messages hidden within these stirring tales.

White Fire

When a young Native American girl suddenly finds herself fighting to save her best friend's life, she discovers something amazing about herself.

The Appaloosa Colt

An eleven-year-old girl who collects model horses has a life-changing encounter with the real thing!

The Horse Whisperer Academy

Katie's scholarship to The Horse Whisperer Academy is a dream come true until she discovers that the other kids are determined to do everything they can to make her life miserable.

Bonus Book Excerpt: *Saving Bluestone Belle*

For your reading pleasure, we are also pleased to present a delightful excerpt from Strawberry Shakespeare's horse-themed, comic-adventure novel, ***Saving Bluestone Belle.*** This award-winning book tells about Homer Easton, a ten-year-old horse-loving kid who hits the road to rescue his beloved horse, Blue, from thieves. In Chapter 10, "Truck Eats," Homer has been kidnapped by the bumbling desperadoes and must find a way to escape and get help for Blue before it's too late!

About Diamond Star Press

At Diamond Star Press we are committed to bringing you the best in children's fiction. We care about your child's interest in reading and are dedicated to encouraging children to read more books. We also believe that books can bring parents and kids together. To that end, we aim to publish stories that are suitable for the whole family, stories that parents and teachers alike will love to read aloud to the children in their lives.

Who Was C. J. Dennis?

C. J. Dennis (Clarrie or Den as he was known to friends and family) was born in Auburn, South Wales, Australia in 1876 to parents of Irish descent. He published his first poem when he was just 19, and throughout his 61 years produced some of the most memorable and funny poetry and books in the English language.

Settling in the pretty town of Adelaide in 1905, Den became editor of the local newspaper and began writing profusely. His sense of humor and wit were apparent to all around him; that special brand of antipodean humor. It was often at work in the oddest of situations. For example, while camping in Toolangi with his friend, artist Hal Waugh, he decided to name their tents "Hall of

Hal" and "Den of Den," pursuing his penchant for funny names into his own daily routine.

Den was clearly influenced by the unique culture of his native country, Australia. A former colony of Great Britain, Australia was also home to an ancient race known as the Aborigines. Their distinctive language stimulated his creative side, as witnessed by the long, unusual names and words in some of his later works for children.

C. J. Dennis wrote for more than forty years, and it is thought that he penned about 4000 pieces of prose and poetry, easily making him one of the most productive writers of all time. He had a wild imagination and a sense of humor to match, appealing to people of all ages. Though he began his career as a journalist, he soon was writing books and poems for both adults and children.

In 1915, Dennis bought a piece of land and started building a house called "Arden." He planted a garden around it in which he could work, and it was there, nestled amongst the garden and the log house, that he began his most important period of writing.

At first, Den wrote solely for an adult audience. His best-known work, *Songs of a Sentimental Bloke,* was read and recorded all over the world, and spoke to the average person. But it was his effortless style and genius in his children's books, such as *The Glugs of Gosh* (1917) and his famous *A Book for Kids* (1921) that cemented his popularity.

Dennis never had children of his own, but he got the idea of writing for children when he found out that one of his friend's sons was hurt in an accident and had to spend time in hospital. Dennis thought that the best thing for the youngster would be a cheerful and entertaining book about a wonderful land and strange people called the Glugs. In fact, *The Glugs of Gosh* became so popular that even adults were counted as fans of his children's books.

C. J. Dennis' special gift was his ability to make people laugh through his hilarious poems. *A Book for Kids* is just this: a collection of poems and short stories, designed to make you laugh, wonder and enter the magical worlds he creates. Dennis knew that we all have a child inside, and in the dedication he aimed his work at everyone "over four and under four-and-eighty."

He even went so far as to illustrate *A Book for Kids* with his own drawings, often having some funny stories to tell about the process. One story concerned his drawing of a baby. He couldn't get the feet right, and drew the baby's big toes on the outside of the feet. When his wife asked him about it, he replied that he knew very little about babies anyway! Initially, the title of the volume was *A Book of Illustrated Nonsense Verse,* which is the name he used in a letter to his friend James Tyrell. But he changed the title to *A Book for Kids,* the name it is best known by today, even though it was changed once again in 1935 to *Roundabout.*

A Book for Kids contains poems and stories aimed at brightening up anyone's day. "The Triantiwontigongolope" is a favorite among all ages, especially kids who love trying to pronounce the name in different ways. It's a comical poem about an imaginary insect called a Triantiwontigongolope who lives in a magical land where "the trees and grass were purple, and the sky bottle green." Another favorite is "The Boy Who Rode into the Sunset," a colorful saga about a little boy who flies around the world on the back of a white horse and meets all sorts of strange characters, like the Head Scene-Shifter and the Last Sunbeam.

Den's works for children fired up the imagination and made adults and kids laugh at a time when the world was still recovering from World War I while beginning its descent into the Great Depression. Parents distracted themselves by reading Dennis' poems and stories to their children and discussing their meaning. Children loved to imagine the wonderful descriptions in the book, and enjoyed drawing their own makeshift Triantiwonti-gongolopes on purple grass!

"The Circus" is another poem where Den describes, in a few verses, acrobats swinging, dappled horses galloping and dogs jumping through hoops—all the memories of going to the circus summed up in a short poem.

Dennis' books offer a lighter side that, in his era, was often absent from children's books. He manages to lighten the mood and get everyone interested in his new animals and worlds full of funny things. There are places called Cuppacumalonga, ridiculous riddles like

Woolloomooloo, barbers "going snip snip snip" and even an old horse called Dobbin.

Another favorite is the poem "Growing Up" from *A Book for Kids,* about Little Tommy Tadpole. In just a few lines, Den captures the essence of growing up:

"Little Tommy Tadpole began to weep and wail,
For little Tommy Tadpole had lost his little tail;
And his mother didn't know him as he wept upon a log,
For he wasn't Tommy Tadpole, but Mr. Thomas Frog."

Den's poetry for children comes alive when read aloud, and in his day, children loved to sing along with his poems, learn the funny words and play out the characters; like "The Ant" going on his adventure, climbing his six inch mountain and crossing the "dreadful desert" that was just a few feet wide. Kids could put themselves in the ant's shoes and imagine how trekking only a few feet might seem so very hard and long if you are a little ant who is out to explore the world on your own.

Throughout his life, Den suffered from poor health, yet despite this he managed to write prolifically. When he died, the Australian Prime Minister at the time compared him to the great Scottish poet Robert Burns and commented that Dennis left behind a legacy that will be enjoyed by everyone.

Read on for "The Cloud Horse," a novelette by Strawberry Shakespeare based on the short story, "The Boy Who Rode into the Sunset" by C. J. Dennis, from his children's classic, *A Book for Kids*.

The Cloud Horse

An exhilarating tale about a kid who is whisked away on the back of a flying horse!

It Comes Down from Above!

Once upon a time—it was not so very long ago, either—a little boy, named Neville, lived with his people in a house which was almost in the country. That is to say, it was just at the edge of the city; and at the back of the house was a rather large hill, which was quite bald.

Neville, who was fond of playing by himself, would often wander to the top of the bald hill; and if he stood right on top of it and looked one way, toward the east, he could see right over the city, with all its tall buildings and domes and spires and smoking chimneys. But looking the other way, to the west, he could see for miles over the beautiful country, with its green fields and orchards and white roads and little farm houses.

One evening Neville was playing alone on the top of the hill when he noticed that one of the very finest sunsets he had ever seen was just coming on. The sky in the west, away over the broad country lands, was filled with little clouds of all sorts and shapes, and they were just beginning to take on the most wonderful colors.

Neville had often before amused himself with watching clouds and the strange shapes into which they changed themselves--sometimes like great mountain ranges, sometimes like sea-waves, and very often like elephants and lions and seals and all manner of interesting things of that sort. But never before had he been able to make out so many animal shapes in the clouds. The sky was almost as good as a zoo. There were kangaroos and elephants and a hen with chickens and wallabies and rabbits and a funny man with large ears and all sorts of other peculiar shapes.

The sun was sinking behind a distant range of hills, where a golden light shone out as if through a gateway. It was so much like a great golden gateway that Neville fell to wondering what might be found on the other side of it.

Suddenly, right in the middle of all the colored clouds, he saw one little cloud which was perfectly white, and, as he watched it, he noticed that it seemed to be shaped like a small horse. A very small horse it seemed at that distance; but, as Neville gazed, it grew bigger and bigger, just as if it were coming toward him very fast, and he was almost certain he could see its legs moving.

That startled him a little, and so he rubbed his eyes to make sure that they were not playing him tricks. When he looked again he was more startled than ever; for the little white cloud was no longer a cloud, but a little white horse in real earnest. Besides, it had just left the sky and was galloping down the mountain range which he could see away in the west.

In two minutes it had left the range, and was coming across the fields towards him, jumping the fences, dodging under the trees, and racing across the plain with its white mane and tail tossing as it came. It seemed to be making straight for him.

He was not really frightened—you must not think that about him—but he was just beginning to wonder if it were not nearly time to go home to dinner, when he noticed that the white horse had stopped, just at the foot of the bald hill. It was looking up at him, tossing its head and pawing the ground—the most beautiful white horse that he had ever seen, even in a circus. Then it appeared to get over its excitement and began to trot quietly up the hill toward him.

Meet the Cloud Horse

I do not think anyone would have blamed Neville if he had decided then to go home to dinner at once. But he was rather a brave boy, and he was certainly very curious, so he just stood still and waited.

And here is where the most wonderful part of the story begins. The white horse trotted up to Neville and spoke to him. That would surprise most people; and Neville was certainly as much surprised as anyone else would have been.

"What are you frightened of?" asked the white horse in a loud voice.

Now, Neville WAS just a little frightened by this time; but he was not going to show it, so he just said, "Who's frightened?"

"YOU'RE frightened," said the white horse, louder than ever. "You're only a timid little boy. I thought when I saw you in the distance that you were one of the plucky ones; but I was mistaken. You're just a little cowardly-custard."

"You'd better be careful who you're talking to," said Neville, suddenly losing his fear. (Little boys do not always talk good grammar; otherwise he would have said "whom" not "who.") He hated to be called a "cowardly-custard." "You'd better be careful, or I'll give you a bang!"

"Ah ha!" cried the white horse. "Very brave all at once, aren't you? All the same, you're afraid to come near and stroke me."

"But I don't want to stroke you," said Neville.

"I thought not," replied the white horse. "I thought not, the moment I got close to you. You're one of the frightened ones, and I've been wasting my time."

"Who's frightened?" said Neville again.

"You asked that before," replied the white horse, "and I told you. If you're not frightened, come along and stroke me. There's nothing to be afraid of."

So Neville walked right up to the white horse and stroked his shoulder. And at once he felt that he had been foolish to hold back. For of all the smooth, soft, silky coats he had ever stroked, that of the white horse was certainly the smoothest, and the softest, and the silkiest. He felt that he could go on stroking it for hours.

"There now," said the white horse in a voice as soft and silky as his coat. "There was nothing to be afraid of, was there? And I think that perhaps I was mistaken about you. I rather think you might be one of those daring boys that one reads about in stories. What about jumping on my back for a little ride?"

Neville ceased to stroke the white horse and drew back a little.

"I'm afraid they'll be expecting me home for dinner," he said. "I'm very pleased indeed to have met you." Neville was always a polite little boy.

"The very thing!" cried the white horse. "Jump on my back and I'll take you home. You liked stroking me, didn't you? Well that's nothing compared to the ride you will enjoy—simply nothing. Why, all the boldest riders in the world would give their ears just for one little ride on my back. Now then! One, two, three, and up you go!"

Then before Neville quite knew what he was doing, he made a little run and leapt up astride of the white horse

"I live just over there," said Neville, pointing towards his home.

But before he could say "knife," or even "scissors" (supposing he had wished to say either of these words), the white horse laughed a nasty hollow laugh, sprang upwards from the ground, and was soaring through the air toward the dying sunset, right away from home and dinner.

Neville's First Flight

Neville clung on tightly, for he was so high above the earth that to fall off would mean the end of him. And far beneath him he saw the green fields and the white road, which now seemed like a mere thread.

"That's not fair! Whoa back! Whoa back!" he shouted to the white horse; but the white horse made no reply. Indeed, he seemed suddenly not so much like a white horse as like a white cloud shaped like a horse, and Neville saw that he no longer sat upon the horse's silky coat, but upon something soft and downy like a white fleece, and it was slightly damp. Then he knew that he was riding upon a cloud; and, as it was quite absurd to go on talking to a cloud, he ceased to cry out. He just sat tight and wondered what would happen next.

He was high over a farmhouse now: one that he used to see from the bald hill. He knew it by the tall pine trees that grew round it; and down in the farmyard he saw a man with a bucket going out to feed the calves. Neville called loudly to him, but the man did not even look up.

Now he was far beyond that farmhouse and above an orchard, where he saw the fruit trees standing in straight rows; and a few seconds later the mountain range was beneath him, and Neville knew that the cloud that looked like a horse was making straight for the golden gateway, which was now glowing dully in a gray sky. He was riding into the sunset.

Swiftly as the wind that drove it, the Cloud Horse drifted over the mountain range. There was a sudden glow of golden light all about him, and then a flash of color so wonderful that Neville could not bear to look. He closed his eyes, and, as he did so, he felt that the Cloud Horse had come to a halt at last.

So Neville sat upon the cloud, not daring to open his eyes for quite a long time. When at last he did look again he almost fainted with the wonder of it. He was inside the sunset.

The Last Sunbeam and the Head Scene-Shifter

But scarcely had he begun to enjoy the wonderful sight, when he was startled by the sound of a funny, shrill little voice close by his side. Looking down, he saw a strange little man, no taller than a walking stick, and dressed from top to toe in golden-yellow clothes.

"My stars!" said the wee yellow man. "How did YOU manage to get in here? Don't you know this is private?"

"I'm very sorry," said Neville, "but I couldn't help it. The Cloud Horse brought me, you know."

"Ah!" said the wee yellow man. "He tricked you, did he? He's much too playful, that Cloud Horse; and, I must say, he's put you in a pretty fix."

"Excuse me," said Neville, "but do you mind telling me who you are?"

"I?" cried the little yellow man. "Why, I'm the Last Sunbeam, of course. I thought you knew that. My job, you know, is to shut up the show when the sunset is over. And it's pretty hard work, I can tell you, because I've got to keep on doing it all round the earth every few minutes or so. And it gets very tiresome at times. Would you believe it? I've never seen a dawn or a bright midday in all my life—just sunsets all the time. Sunsets for breakfast, sunsets for dinner, sunsets for supper. And if I make the tiniest little slip, the head scene-shifter is down on me like a ton of bricks."

"Goodness me!" said Neville. "I didn't know you had scene-shifters here." Neville had been to see pantomimes, and therefore knew what a scene-shifter was.

"Then how do you think we shift the scenes?" cried the wee yellow man rather crossly. Then he suddenly became very busy about nothing, as he whispered, "Look out! Here's the head scene-shifter coming now."

Looking back, Neville saw, coming towards them, a man with very large ears. He was not a nice-looking man, and he was extremely like the cloud man that Neville had sometimes seen in the sky when he went to look at the sunset from the bald hill.

"Now then! Now then!" roared the man with the large ears. "Move yourself there, Goldie! We shut up the show here in a few minutes, and open at once on the next range. See that you have that curtain down on time."

"Certainly, sir," replied the little yellow man very humbly.

Then the man with the large ears noticed Neville for the first time. He frowned darkly, and his big ears seemed to flap with annoyance.

"Who is this on our Cloud Horse?" he roared in his great angry voice.

"Just a little boy," said the yellow man—for Neville was far too frightened to speak. "Just a little boy that the Cloud Horse has been playing tricks on. I think he'd like to be getting home—just over by the bald hill, if you don't mind, sir."

"Certainly not!" shouted the man with the large ears. "The Cloud Horse is not to go out there again tonight, nor the silly little boy either. I'm not going to have the sunset upset by any such silly nonsense. You mind what I say and attend to your work."

And, without another glance at Neville, the man with the large ears strode off to arrange for the sunset on the next range, miles and miles away.

The Sky Flower

Neville gazed at the wee yellow man hopelessly, and the wee yellow man gazed at Neville, and neither spoke a word until the man with the large ears was well out of the way. Then the Last Sunbeam grew quite cheerful again.

"Well," said he, "you heard what the head sceneshifter said. You certainly can't go home by the way you came. The only thing for you to do is to go round. You'll just about have time to do it, if you hurry."

"Go round?" repeated Neville in a puzzled voice. "Go round what, round where?"

"Round the world, of course," replied the little yellow man.

"Round the world?" cried Neville. "Why you must be making fun of me, and I think that is very unkind."

"Not a bit of it," laughed the little yellow man. "You need not make such a fuss about it. Why, I go round the world once every day with the sunset. You have only to go a bit faster so as to do it in a few minutes, and with the Cloud Horse to help you that's easily managed. Don't you worry about the Cloud Horse, he has got to do just whatever I tell him. Now, excuse me for one moment and I'll give you full directions."

With that the wee yellow man went behind a pink cloud and came back with a beautiful blue flower in his hand.

"This," he said, handing the flower to Neville, "is a Sky Flower. It is made entirely out of a genuine piece of sky, and it is a talisman—that's a longer word for charm, you know—which takes you free round the world. The one thing you have to remember is that you mustn't, on any account, lose that flower until you get home again. Now, just exactly what you have to do is to travel west and race round the world until you catch up with this evening again. It is quite simple."

"Simple!" cried Neville. "Why I don't understand it at all."

"Dear me!" said the wee yellow man rather impatiently, "you are very dense. Now listen carefully. The world, you know, turns round from west to east, and that makes it seem as if the sun is going round the world from east to west. Very well. So what you have to do is to ride west upon the Cloud Horse much faster than the sun appears to travel, and catch him up again before he gets well away from here. The Cloud Horse is in good condition, and you should easily do it in a few minutes."

"A few minutes!" gasped Neville.

"Keep quiet and listen," snapped the wee yellow man. "A few miles west from here you will come into broad daylight. That will be afternoon. After that you will meet midday, and, passing that, you will reach the place where it is only dawn. That's about halfway round the earth. Show the Sky Flower to the Porter of the Dawn, and he will let you through. Then you get to the half of the world where it is night, and you must race round that till you reach the place where it is only evening. That will be THIS evening, somewhere about here, for you will have taken only a few minutes altogether. And when you see your own home or the bald hill again, grasp the Sky Flower tightly in your hand, jump off the Cloud Horse, and you will float gracefully down to the earth. It won't hurt you. Then you can go home, and I hope you will not be late for dinner."

"But," began Neville, "I can't understand—"

"My time is valuable," said the wee yellow man, as he shook hands. "Goodbye and a pleasant journey." With that he smacked the Cloud Horse smartly on the flank, and in a moment it was racing into the west at a most terrific pace.

Racing Round the World

Of course, now that airplanes have been invented, flying is not thought so wonderful as once it was. But loafing along through the air in a biplane or a monoplane at eighty or a hundred miles an hour is a very tame business when you compare it with racing the day round the world on a Cloud Horse. And Neville is very probably the only person who has ever done that yet.

Almost before he knew what had happened, he had left evening far behind and was riding in broad daylight. The Cloud Horse had ridden high in the air, and Neville saw the broad country, with plains and hills and forest lands, stretched far beneath him. An instant later, and the land was no longer below him, but the wide sea, sparkling in brilliant sunlight.

Before he had time to notice very much he had reached midday, high over a strange foreign land, and was racing through the morning toward the dawn. So quickly did he go that there was little chance of seeing anything clearly; but he had glimpses of many strange sights; many ships he saw upon the sea—small ships and stately steamers crawling over the ocean like strange water-beetles. Once, as the Cloud Horse drifted low, Neville saw a beautiful sailing ship, with all sails set, and strange-looking men upon the deck. They looked very like pirates, and perhaps they were; but Neville had no time to make sure, for the very next minute he was over a wild land where he saw a horde of black men, with spears and clubs, hunting an elephant through a clearing in a great jungle. As he looked, the elephant turned to charge the hunters; but what happened then Neville did not see, for in a moment more he was above a great city with crowds of people in the streets—people dressed in strange, bright-colored clothes—and there were bells ringing and whistles blowing. Then a great desert spread beneath him, with no living thing in sight but a great tawny lion prowling over the sand. Then came the sea again, and more ships; and the light began to grow dim, for he was nearly halfway round the earth, and was approaching the dawn.

Dimmer grew the light, and dimmer yet, just as though evening were coming—and before him, Neville saw the dawn like a silvery gateway in the sky. Straight toward it the Cloud Horse rushed, and stopped so suddenly that Neville almost fell off.

"What's all this? What's all this?" cried a small voice; and Neville saw beside the silver gateway, a little man dressed from top to toe in silver gray. It was the Porter of the Dawn, sometimes called the First Sunbeam.

Before Neville could answer, the little gray man had caught sight of the Sky Flower.

"Ah, you have the talisman," said he. "Pass in! And don't stop to gossip, because I'm very busy this morning. A pleasant journey," he added as he smacked the Cloud Horse on the shoulder; and in an instant Neville had passed through the dawn and plunged into the night.

Flying in the Dark

It was a dark night, with no moon, for the sky was overcast with dense clouds. Above these the Cloud Horse flew, and overhead Neville saw the rushing stars, and below only the blackness of heavy clouds. But more often the Cloud Horse flew low, and then there was little to be seen. By the lights of moving ships Neville knew that sometimes he was above the sea. Sometimes twinkling lights in towns or solitary farms, or the sudden blaze of a great city told him that the land was beneath him.

Once, through the blackness, he saw a great forest fire upon an island, and the light of it lit up the sea, and showed the natives crowded upon the beach and in the shallows, and some making off in canoes.

Then darkness swallowed the Cloud Horse again, and the blazing island was left far behind.

After that, Neville began to feel a little drowsy. Perhaps he did sleep a little, for the next thing he saw was a faint light in the sky before him, as though the dawn were coming. But he knew it must be the evening, because he was coming back to the place from which he had started, and was catching up with the sun. You see, he had only been gone a few minutes.

The Cloud Horse flew very low now; and rapidly the darkness grew less. Then, long before he expected it, Neville saw the roof of his own home below him. He could see the garden in the twilight and his own dog sniffing about among the trees as though in search of him.

Neville began to think about jumping now, and he was rather nervous. He might land softly and he might not. He only had the wee yellow man's word for that.

Then, to his horror, he saw that they had passed his home and were over the bald hill. There was no time to lose. The Cloud Horse was taking him into the sunset again, and, if he did, what would the head scene-shifter say then?

So, grasping the Sky Flower very tightly, Neville closed his eyes and jumped. He half expected to fall quickly and be dashed to pieces upon the earth; but, instead, he floated in the air like a feather, swaying and drifting, and slowly sinking all the time towards the ground. It was a very pleasant sensation indeed.

Home Sweet Home

The bald hill was beneath him as he came slowly down, down, down. He could see the Cloud Horse—now little more than a small white speck—rushing on to catch the sunset. And still he sank down ever so slowly towards the top of the bald hill.

His little dog had caught sight of him now, and came rushing out the gate and up the bald hill, barking loudly. And he kept on sinking nearer to the earth, down, down, nearer and nearer—and then, quite suddenly, he seemed to forget everything.

The next thing Neville remembered was feeling something wet and warm upon his cheek. He opened his eyes and saw that the little dog was licking his face. Sitting up, he looked about him. He was in the grass on the top of the bald hill; night was very near, and the first star was just beginning to twinkle.

Then, quite suddenly, Neville remembered the Cloud Horse and the little yellow man and the little silver man and the head scene-shifter and the wonderful journey and all the rest of it.

"Well, what a remarkable dream," said Neville, stretching his arms. And, as he did so, the Sky Flower fell from his hand.

So it was not a dream after all; for, if it was, how could he explain that Sky Flower? He picked it up and carried it very tenderly, as he set off home to dinner, his little dog trotting at his heels.

"What a beautiful flower!" said Neville's mother when he got home. "Where ever did you get it?"

"It is a piece of the genuine sky," said Neville proudly, as he gave it to her.

His mother smiled at him as she said, "That is a very nice thing to say, and it certainly does look like a little piece of the sky. But, of course, it couldn't possibly be a real piece."

Then Neville knew that if he were to tell the story of his wonderful ride, and tried to explain that he had been right around the world since he went out to play, his parents would find it very, very hard to believe. So he said nothing, but ate a very good dinner.

But Neville's mother put the flower in a vase upon the mantel; and to this day it is still there, as fresh and bright as ever. It will not fade. Neville's mother thinks that is a very strange and wonderful thing. And so it is.

Since that day, when Neville goes to the top of the bald hill to watch a sunset, he is almost sure that, just as the golden light is fading, he can see a little yellow man by the gateway; and it seems to him that the little yellow man waves a cheery greeting. But, whether this is so or not, Neville always waves back; and he feels very happy to think that he has a good friend inside the sunset.

White Fire

When a young Native American girl suddenly finds herself fighting to save her best friend's life, she discovers something amazing about herself.

Singing Bird gathered wood in the forest. Her beautiful voice rang out in the stillness, clear and true. She loved the way her voice echoed in the canyons. She loved the way it soared across the plains as if on wing. But most of all, she loved to sing in the forest where the wind in the trees, the birds on the branches and the footsteps of invisible creatures created an exquisite harmony.

"Singing Bird." Her mother's distant voice broke the stillness. The young girl hurried to the clearing where her mother waited with a worried face.

"Where have you been? Did you not hear me call?"

"I am sorry, Mother."

"Next time, stay closer to camp."

"Yes, Mother."

"Ah, you did well." The woman took the large pile of wood and brought it to the rear of the teepee.

"Now help me chop these for the stew." She handed the girl a bowl of potatoes and a wooden knife.

Singing Bird cut the potatoes into bite-size chunks then placed them in the simmering pot. At that moment,

Running Deer darted by with a big grin on her face. Singing Bird looked after her with longing.

"Mother, may I go with Running Deer?"

Her mother took the knife from Singing Bird and said gently, "Go, Daughter, but be back before the setting of the sun."

Singing Bird raced away to join her friend by the lake.

Running Deer was up to her knees in water. "Come in. It feels so good."

Singing Bird did not waste a moment to wade toward her friend, enjoying the tepid liquid against her skin.

"Ow!" screamed Running Deer.

"What is it?"

Running Deer gasped for air and fell backwards into the water, her eyes wide with shock.

Singing Bird quickly raised the girl's head, keeping her face above water, and pulled her out of the lake.

While her friend lay unconscious, Singing Bird stood and cupped her hands around her mouth to signal the tribe.

"Whip-poor-will! Whip-poor-will! Whip-poor-will!" she half-called, half-whistled, her voice careening high and low.

She bent down and lovingly caressed Running Deer's face. "Don't worry, my friend, help is on the way." But after a few minutes passed and no one came, Singing Bird realized that the others could not hear her signal.

Noticing a red wound on Running Deer's left foot, Singing Bird recognized the bite of a deadly water moccasin! The foot had swollen to twice its normal size.

She fell to her knees and began vigorously sucking the venom out of the wound. She did this repeatedly, spitting the venom out each time, until she could do no more.

Exhausted, Singing Bird rested by the lake with Running Deer's head in her lap, and watched the sun set. It was her favorite time—the blue hour—and she felt her strength return.

Suddenly a melody began to grow deep inside her. Never before had such sounds come from the girl as she lifted her chin toward the sky.

Her voice possessed an unearthly resonance that caused the wind in the trees, the birds on the branches and all the invisible creatures to freeze in time.

As if by magical force, sounds tore out of her until Singing Bird felt herself immersed in a shimmering stream of light. Lifted to her feet, she watched the trees flare, and the craggy rocks, the dry ground, the lake itself, explode into blue-white electricity.

Lying on the shore, Running Deer was ablaze in a fire so bright, Singing Bird had to look away lest she scorch her eyes. But there was no escape. Where once were trees and brush and rock and lake, a white fire now burned, illuminating the sky.

Singing Bird felt a tap tap tap on her shoulder. She turned, her eyes like stars. Through the radiance, she smiled at her brothers, whom she knew would come.

Running Deer was already standing, yet she seemed dazed. Looking at the girl's foot, Singing Bird saw that the red, broken skin and purple swelling had completely disappeared.

With a faraway gleam in her eyes, Running Deer embraced her friend. "You saved my life. I was cold, so very cold. How did you make that fire? We had no wood." Puzzled, Running Deer stared at Singing Bird who shrugged, having no answer.

To anyone who would listen, Running Deer would tell how she was bitten by a poisonous snake and how Singing Bird saved her by summoning a strange white fire.

From that day forth, Singing Bird was called White Fire. She studied with the old medicine man who taught her his healing secrets. After his death, White Fire became the medicine woman of her tribe and was known far and wide for her great gift of healing.

The Appaloosa Colt

An eleven-year-old girl who collects model horses has a life-changing encounter with the real thing!

Katie eagerly thumbed through the money her mother handed to her. She had been waiting all week to receive it.

As she ran to the front door, her mother called after her in a stern tone, "Aren't you forgetting something?"

Katie spun around with a sheepish smile. "Thank you!" She waved the folded bills at her mother and raced out the door.

A few months earlier, after Katie's eleventh birthday, her mother decided to give her a weekly allowance for completing chores. The girl used every penny she received to fund her ever-growing collection of model horses. Her older brother, Max, called them toys, but they were much more than that.

The sun on her face felt glorious as Katie sped downtown on her bike. She pumped hard through the turn onto Main Street, and then slid to a stop in front of Williams Mercantile.

Katie peered through the store window at the newest model on display; a perfect miniature replica of an Appaloosa horse, right down to the white snowflake-like spots on its dark coat. She admired it for a moment longer, and then hurried into the shop.

Mr. Williams smiled when he saw her enter. "Katie, I was wondering if you would be in today." He was quite used to her visits and enjoyed seeing her. She had a true passion for the model horses, and he knew it was not just because they were pretty, but because they also represented the freedom and nobility of the real thing.

Katie thought the most ideal way to live her life would be on the back of a horse, riding off into the sunset. Of course, her life was in the suburbs, with plenty of sunsets, but very few horses. That was why she enjoyed collecting the miniatures; even if she couldn't ride them, she could surround herself with them and dream of what it would be like.

"I see you have the Appaloosa," Katie said with a polite smile. Her fingers were wiggling against the legs of her jeans as she itched to get her hands on it. She held her breath while Mr. Williams, who was in his eighties, fumbled with the lock on the glass display case. When he removed the tiny horse, Katie was amazed by its details.

It seemed so real, from the muscles beneath its coat, to the gleam in its dark eyes.

"I think I have enough," she announced, pulling her money out of her pocket and plunking it down on the counter.

While the shopkeeper wrapped the horse and carefully placed it inside a small box, Katie caught sight of a sign taped onto the counter. It advertised a volunteer program at a local horse rescue. She stared at the pictures of horses on the flyer, her heart pounding. "Is there an age limit for this?"

"No, ma'am," Mr. Williams said with a smile as he tucked her money into the register and handed her the box containing her horse. "If you volunteer the time, they'll find a way for you to help." He gave her a copy of the flyer.

Katie was so excited she almost forgot to say 'thank you.' At the door she paused and grinned over her shoulder. "Thanks!"

Mr. Williams smiled as he watched her climb onto her bike and zip away.

When Katie arrived home, she spoke so quickly her mother held up her hand to slow her down. "Wait, wait," she pleaded with a little laugh. "Start again, and slower."

"There's a volunteer program at the horse rescue, and they take kids!" Katie exclaimed. "Please, Mom, will you let me?"

Her mother frowned. She worried about her daughter's safety around such large animals. But then she noticed the new box in the girl's hands, and knew there was nothing Katie would enjoy more than helping the animals she loved so much.

"All right," her mother said, "if you promise to be careful."

"Oh, I will!" Katie cried.

That night as the girl lay in bed, she could not think of anything but the next afternoon. Her mother had called the number on the flyer and made arrangements for her to start right away. She was so happy, she thought she might burst with joy.

Along with four other miniature horses, the Appaloosa stood proudly in the moonlight that spilled through the curtains on Katie's window. His dark coat glimmered, and the speckles of white that dotted it seemed to glow. Katie smiled at the horse as she finally fell asleep.

When she arrived at the horse rescue center the next day, she couldn't wait to see the horses. Instead, she was taken on a tour of the main building by a woman named Marsha, who was dressed like a cowboy, from the boots on her feet to the Stetson on her head. Katie was glad to see everything, including the special medical facilities for the horses and the library full of information, but she kept glancing out the windows.

"So," the woman said with a grin, as she spotted Katie looking out the window for the thousandth time, "are you ready to meet the horses?"

Katie nodded so quickly that her ginger curls bounced against her cheeks.

Marsha led Katie out through a back door. There was a large horse paddock and beyond it were the stalls.

Before Marsha allowed Katie into the stalls, she told her the rules one more time. "Do not try to ride the horses. Only touch or care for the horses that have a green sign on their stalls, never the red." She looked into Katie's eyes to be sure she understood. "Most of the horses are very friendly, but some are wild." As if to prove her point, a horse whinnied loudly.

Finally, they headed to the stalls. When Katie saw the horses, she squealed with pleasure and ran from one to the other. "An Arabian!" she pointed out. "Oh, and a Clydesdale!"

Katie stopped suddenly as she reached a stall with a red sign on it. She did not get too close to the stall but stood on her toes so she could see inside.

"Is that really an Appaloosa?" she asked breathlessly.

"Yes," Marsha said, catching up with her. "But she just foaled, so we mustn't disturb her."

Katie nodded in agreement. "Was it a filly or a colt?" she inquired, as she could not see a foal inside the stall.

"A colt," the woman said proudly. "Okay, I'd like you to start by organizing the grooming area. Do you think you can?"

"Of course!" Katie replied with determination.

After giving her a quick overview, Marsha left the girl alone to work. As she diligently carried out her assignment, Katie felt lucky to be around real horses.

When she finished, she could not resist one more peek at the horses. She greeted each one cheerfully, and then lingered a bit in front of the stall with the Appaloosa. She wanted to see the foal so badly.

As she stood on her tiptoes hoping to catch a glimpse of it, she noticed that the stall door was not closed properly. When she stepped closer, she saw that it was open wide enough for a small colt to slip through. She knew she wasn't supposed to go into the stalls with the red signs, but she was worried that maybe the colt had escaped.

She carefully pulled open the door to the stall. Inside, the large mare was resting. Her coat was dark in color and flecked with white splotches on her hindquarters.

"I-I am here to help," Katie stammered. She had never been so close to a horse before.

As she inched into the stall, the mare, who was known to be testy, gazed at her with calm eyes. But there was no sign of a colt anywhere!

Alarmed, Katie closed the stall door behind her. She rushed out of the barn and was running back toward the main building when she heard a soft whinny. She stopped in her tracks and turned to look in the direction of the sound, just in time to catch a glimpse of a small colt disappearing into the woods.

He was so young, and Katie was certain he would get lost. She didn't know what to do. Should she run to the building for help and hope that the colt would still be close enough to be found? Or should she chase after him before he got too far away?

Katie took off after the colt. As she ran, she imagined she was a horse, with her muscles flexing, and her powerful legs propelling her as swiftly as the wind that blew through her hair.

Once in the woods, she searched for any sign of the colt. She knew he would be afraid and wanting his mother; he was only a few days old.

The woods grew darker as the sun began to set. She had been searching for quite some time and was ready to give up, when she saw him out of the corner of her eye.

He was beautiful, with a glossy black coat and white snowflakes splashed all over him, just like the miniature she had at home.

"It's okay," she whispered as she crept closer to him. The young colt backed away from her and whinnied.

"Shh," she whispered, "I'm here to help you." Her voice was warm and comforting as it enveloped him.

She reached her hand out to him with her palm facing the darkening sky. She had to get the horse to trust her because the woods would soon be pitch black, and she might not be able to find her way out. It was then she realized she had no idea what she was doing. She had never touched a real horse, let alone wrangled a colt. She knew that if she was nervous he might sense it, so she took a deep breath and did her best to be brave.

The colt hesitantly nudged her palm with his nose, drawn in by her scent and the warmth she exuded. With gentle hands she began to stroke his coat. She could feel him trembling.

"I know I look strange, and I probably smell very different," she murmured to the horse. "It's okay to be afraid, but if you trust me, I can get you home to your mother." As her palms glided along the foal's coat, she could feel his heart pounding. Katie imagined how afraid she would be if she were lost with no idea how to get home.

As she stroked the colt, she hummed softly in a steady, smooth rhythm. When she felt his heartbeat slow down and he was no longer shivering, she knew it was time to get him home. But Katie had nothing with her to loop around the colt's neck, and he was far too heavy for her to lift and carry. Then it occurred to her to tell him a story.

"If you walk with me, we share the same sky, and the same ground," she said, taking a step forward.

The colt looked up at her with wide eyes and took a step toward her.

"If you walk with me, no matter how far apart we are, we share the same sky, and the same ground." Katie took a few steps forward, and glanced back to see the colt following behind her.

"We may be different, but our hearts lead us, exactly the same." She smiled at the colt as he appeared beside her. "I don't have to take you to your mother, you can find her yourself. Just follow the guidance of your heart."

At those words, the colt began trotting. Katie kept pace with him, surprised that he seemed to understand her.

She always dreamed of being able to talk to horses and sense what they felt and thought. When she saw how frightened the colt was and thought of how frightened she would be in the same situation, she realized that just because she was a human and the colt was an animal, his thoughts and emotions were not so different. He needed someone he could trust to reassure him that he could never really be lost.

She heard Marsha calling her name from the edge of the woods. Her voice sounded furious and terrified at the same time.

"Over here!" Katie yelled back.

"Katie, what were you thinking?" Marsha said reproachfully as the girl and colt emerged from the brush. Though the sight of the young foal calmly walking alongside Katie amazed her, she was angry he had been let out. “I told you not to touch the horses in the stalls with the red signs. Why did you let him out?”

Marsha's tone was so full of disapproval, Katie felt hot tears of embarrassment and shame form in her eyes. If Marsha didn’t believe her, she would never be able to return to the center and continue to volunteer.

“I didn't let him out,” Katie insisted as Marsha stalked back to the stalls. “He was already out, and I was afraid if I came to get you, he would be lost or hurt in the woods.”

Marsha deposited the colt next to his mother and firmly shut and locked the stall door. Then she turned to the girl with a scowl. “I understand you’re new to horses, Katie, but the colt is only a few days old. He could have been injured or worse. There’s no way he wandered off on his own. I locked the stall earlier, just like I did now.”

She turned back to show Katie how sturdy the lock was, only to discover that the door to the stall had drifted open. “How in the world?” she exclaimed as she pushed on the door. Now she could see that the fastener had become loose, so that even when it was locked, the door would not hold shut. "Oh no!" she gasped, realizing her mistake.

She looked at Katie apologetically. "I really thought it was locked. I'm so sorry."

"It's okay," Katie said with a sigh of relief. "I wasn't sure what to do."

Marsha smiled. "What you did was very brave. I hope you continue to come here, because I think you have a real gift with horses." She thought a moment and then added, "I'll even teach you to ride, if you would like that."

"Oh, yes!" the girl cried, jumping up and down, unable to contain her excitement.

That night in bed, as sleep was descending, Katie smiled at the miniature Appaloosa shimmering in the moonlight. She still loved her tiny horses, but she was so happy her dreams had finally come true.

The Horse Whisperer Academy

12-year-old Katie's summer scholarship to The Horse Whisperer Academy is a dream come true until she discovers that the other kids are determined to do everything they can to make her life miserable.

An old stone house loomed ahead as they rounded the last curve on the steep mountain road. Katie felt the excitement rise inside of her when she spotted the sign on the gate: The Horse Whisperer Academy.

The metal gate creaked open and the driver sped up the long driveway. With a pounding heart, Katie took in the expansive, manicured grounds surrounded by thick forest.

The car stopped at the tall, wooden front door where Katie was greeted by a short, bald-headed man with white whiskers on his chin and a round belly.

"Welcome, Katie!" the round man chortled as he opened the car door with a gleeful smile and assisted her out. "I'm the headmaster, Mr. Wickham."

Katie emerged from the car carrying a small suitcase and followed the headmaster into the house. They went up two sets of winding stairs and down a long, dusty hallway covered with a worn Persian carpet. At the end of the corridor, he unlocked a door and ushered Katie inside.

"This is your room. I hope you like it."

Katie quickly glanced around at the dark brocade curtains covering the window and the matching brocade bedspread on the large, canopied bed. "Oh yes, sir. It's very nice."

"Good!" exclaimed Wickham, "You have a little time to unpack and then we'll see you in the dining room at 6 o'clock on the dot."

Katie nodded, "Yes, sir."

When he turned away and headed to the door, the girl reached for her phone. Without looking back, Wickham said, "You'll have to leave it in the room. We don't get reception here." With that, he left, shutting the door behind him.

Katie flopped down on the edge of the bed, taking in the dark, heavy furnishings, and fell back with a sigh.

The dining room had an oval entranceway from the adjacent sitting room and a very large, rectangular table. When Katie entered, the bubbly conversations, laughter and antics of the six boys and five girls surrounding the table, came to a sudden stop. All eyes turned to Katie who felt her face redden.

A British boy in knickers and a white shirt whispered in the ear of his seatmate to the left and that pink-cheeked rascal whispered in the ear of his seatmate to the left. And so it went, a round of 'telephone' that ended at the pretty, blonde girl on the opposite side of the table. That girl stood up with a haughty expression and said to Katie, "Grover thinks you're odd."

All the kids collapsed in titters and laughter except for Grover, the British boy, who grimaced and shook his head as if to say 'that's not what I said.' At that very moment, Wickham arrived and all the children sat up straight and silent.

"Good evening, children, let me introduce this year's winner of The Horse Whisperer Academy summer scholarship, Katie Winslow. In honor of her arrival she will sit at my right." He gestured to the empty seat, pressing on Katie's back, and the girl went to her place, head hanging.

"Now let us eat and enjoy our dinner and then get a good night's rest because tomorrow is going to be a big day for all of you. We will go out to the stables and visit the horses where you will meet your personal horse and receive your first lesson."

Katie could barely eat dinner; her stomach was doing flip-flops. All the while, the other kids gulped down their food and chattered incessantly. But no one spoke to her except for Mr. Wickham, who made polite conversation.

Thankful to be alone in her room at last, she sank beneath the covers, missing the horse miniatures on her bedroom windowsill that shimmered in the moonlight until she fell asleep.

The next day at the stables, Katie was assigned a dark brown rescue mustang named Godile. He was so much bigger than the old mare she was allowed to ride as a volunteer at the local rescue. How would she control this creature who not long ago galloped the wild plains with the scent of sage rushing past his nostrils?

The kids assembled outside with their horses while Wickham, looking silly in a green plaid riding outfit with matching cap, stood before them. "First you must earn your horse's trust. Now mount your horse."

Katie was terrified as she mounted Godile who seemed irritable, shaking his head at the bit in his mouth and stomping his feet restlessly.

"Today you will take a ride in the forest following that dirt trail." He pointed off to the woods. "Make friends with your horse - that is your first task. Try to understand him. He is always communicating with you, if only you could see with 'horse eyes.' That's right - today, you will try to see with horse eyes, and we shall gather later and discuss your experiences."

The woods were quiet, except for the rustling branches and the occasional squawk of a large bird. It smelled vaguely sweet and damp. The heavy rains had brought the summer foliage out early in lush extreme.

Katie and Godile walked along the trail, enjoying each other's company. Once they were on the trail, he had settled down and Katie was able to encourage him with only the slightest pressure of her knees or tug on the reins. She felt happy to be alive and thrilled to be riding aloft such a magnificent stallion.

Suddenly, Godile's ears twitched and Katie could feel his heart rate increase. Katie knew something was wrong. She spoke to the horse with soothing tones and humming sounds, techniques that worked with the nervous horses at the rescue; but Godile didn't respond. He sped up to a trot though Katie did everything she could to calm him.

As the horse rounded a large tree, Katie spotted the haughty blonde girl, whose name she had learned was Jamie, sprawled on the grass by the side of the trail. Her horse was nowhere to be seen.

Godile slowed down and Katie immediately dismounted, secured the reins to a branch and knelt beside Jamie. "Are you all right, Jamie? Talk to me." But the girl was unresponsive.

Katie felt for a pulse, then got her water canteen and began trickling the cool liquid on Jamie's face, but the girl remained unconscious. Scanning the girl's body, she could see no sign of injury. Still the girl was out cold, and Katie knew she should not move her.

Katie patted Jamie's pale cheeks to see if she could wake her up and poured more water on her face. Finally, the girl's eyes blinked open.

"Where am I?" she gasped. "What happened?"

"Everything's okay, Jamie. You're safe." Katie said, "You must have fallen off your horse."

"Oh, Della," she groused, "that stupid horse. She wouldn't do a thing I said."

Jamie sat up abruptly, rubbing her head, then looked around perplexed. "Where is she?"

"The main thing is to get you back to the house. We'll look for her later."

Katie helped Jamie onto Godile and then mounted and took the reins. The stallion seemed distracted, thrusting his head from side to side. Katie knew he wanted to find Della, but that would have to wait. She stroked his coat and whispered in his ear until he calmed down.

"Can you ride this thing?" Jamie asked as they set off. "It's even bigger than Della."

"Yes, I can," Katie said. "Don't worry about it."

Godile walked slowly to the stone house carrying the two girls. When they arrived, Katie dismounted first and then helped Jamie slide off. She put her arm under the girl's shoulder to support her as they turned to walk to the entrance. At that moment, Wickham came running out with two assistants.

With Jamie resting in the infirmary and under the care of the medical team, Katie was able to think about Della. Horses should not be roaming free in the woods during poaching season. Just as she considered heading out with Godile for a search, Grover, astride a dappled grey mare, emerged from out of the trees holding the reins of Della who passively trotted alongside him.

"Well done!" cried Wickham when the boy and horses arrived at the stables. Katie was nearby, brushing down Godile and struggling to hide her smile and sigh of relief.

Grover slid off his horse. "I found her by the lake," he said, handing Della's reins to Mr. Wickham. "Isn't this Jamie's horse? Where is she?" the boy asked.

Wickham shook his head and said somberly, "The girl fell off the horse and is being looked after. We think she'll be all right. It was Katie who found her and brought her in."

Wickham turned to Katie. "We really appreciate how you helped Jamie. You kept your head and did all the right things." For a moment, he watched her with Godile, noting how she gentled her horse. "And I can see you've made a new friend there."

"You said to learn to see with horse eyes; so I tried to do that," the girl responded. "Godile sensed that some-one was hurt further down the trail before I ever saw Jamie. He also knew that one of the horses was not safe."

"Well done...both of you!" Wickham boomed as he led Della to her stall at the far end of the stables. "Be sure to bring it up at tonight's meeting."

Grover stood there silently, staring at Katie with ad-miration. He loved the way she tossed her long ginger curls when she turned to meet his eyes with her own look of appreciation for his retrieving Della.

In that moment, Katie knew she belonged and that the Horse Whisperer Academy was going to be the best experience of her young life.

Saving Bluestone Belle

BONUS BOOK EXCERPT

In "Truck Eats," Chapter 10 of Strawberry Shakespeare's comic-adventure novel, ***Saving Bluestone Belle,*** ten-year-old Homer has been kidnapped by Rocco and Bart, the bumbling thieves who stole his horse, and must find a way to escape and save Blue before it's too late!

Truck Eats

As their truck barreled down the road in the dead of night, Rocco and Bart noticed a blinking sign: "Truck Eats Restaurant. Next right."

Bart covered Homer's ears. "Eat first, then whack him."

"Whack him, then eat," retorted Rocco.

"Nah," said Bart, "I don't want to risk losing my appetite."

"Suit yourself."

A few minutes later the truck pulled into Truck Eats, and Bart, Rocco and Homer entered the nearly empty restaurant.

"The royals use the john when they can, not when they have to," Rocco informed Bart. "I'll be right back."

Bart mimicked him when he was out of earshot. "Royals-shmoyals, blah, blah, blah."

Bart and Homer took seats at the counter. Bart opened a menu and studied it, but when Homer followed suit, Bart snatched the menu away from him. "You ain't gonna need this where—"

Rocco appeared. He grabbed the menu from Bart and stuck it in Homer's hand. "Idiot," he rasped, "think how it'll look if we eat and the kid doesn't."

A plump, red-faced waitress, wearing a smiley button that said "I'm Waitress Annie, and I love to serve you!" stepped up to the counter. "Hi, folks," she chirped with astonishing good cheer for such an ungodly hour, "thank you for stopping at Truck Eats. What can I get you?"

"I'll have the Saddleman's Stew," said Rocco.

Bart closed his menu. "Same for me. With ketchup."

"You got it," Waitress Annie said, plunking a squirt container of ketchup on the counter. "And you, little man?" she asked Homer with a toothy grin.

The boy cringed as her face loomed above him like a laughing gargoyle. "The Hanged Man's Hotdog with the works."

"Ain't he a card." She ambled away, chuckling.

The men were on Homer like a pooch to the bone. "Try that again, and you're toast," hissed Rocco.

But Waitress Annie had the ears of a rottweiler. She turned. "Want a side of toast?"

Rocco flashed his not-so-pearly whites and nodded.

"White, wheat, or sourdough?"

"White," said Rocco. A muscle in his cheek started twitching.

She scrawled something on her pad and disappeared into the kitchen. Rocco set upon Homer, muttering and gritting his teeth.

Bart jumped up and shook Rocco. "Get a hold of yourself. Don't forget, when this job is over, we're home free."

"I told you we should have done him first," growled Rocco.

Homer tapped Bart's shoulder insistently. "I have to go."

"Hold it in, kid," said Bart.

"I can't. I have to go now." To drive his point home, Homer hopped from foot to foot.

Bart and Rocco exchanged looks and Rocco nodded.

"All right, come on," grumbled Bart, and off they went.

The drab, windowless cell that was the men's restroom at Truck Eats boasted one urinal and two stalls. Bart entered with Homer, who disappeared into the right stall.

"I can't go if anyone is there."

"I can't go if anyone is there," mimicked Bart in a soprano voice. "This is your only chance, kid. Do it or not, I don't care. But I'm not going anywhere."

"Then it'll take a while. Your dinner will get cold."

Bart considered that. "I'll be right outside. Make it fast."

Bart left the restroom and stood by the door, tapping his foot. The waitress winked at him as she passed by with steaming plates of food. He paced back and forth.

Finally he knocked on the door. "Hey kid, hurry it up." But there was only silence. "Kid?"

Bart went inside just as Homer came out of the stall, smiling. A strip of toilet paper trailed from his shoe. At the sight of the twirling paper, Bart heard Rocco's voice intoning, "The royals use the john when they can, not when they have to." After absorbing this profound wisdom, Bart eyed Homer. "Wait here. Don't move, don't even blink."

Homer nodded, still smiling. Bart went into the left stall and stared at the floor while he undid his pants. He settled in, then looked up—and gaped in horror at a message written in ketchup on the back of the door. It read "Help! I've been kidnapped by truck 2KTSO47."

"Aaah!" screamed Bart, jumping up and fixing his pants. He wiped the message off with a wad of toilet paper, threw the paper on the floor, and burst out of the stall.

The air vent grating flapped, but not a kid in sight. Bart got down on his hands and knees, removed the grate, and squeezed in up to his shoulders.

"Grrrr!" roared Bart, spying a moving strand of toilet paper. He felt his face swelling and flushing with rage.

Bart hotfooted it to Rocco, who hunched over the counter, devouring his stew.

"He's gone," squeaked Bart, suddenly losing his voice.

"What!" exploded Rocco. "I leave you alone for one minute—" Rocco dumped Bart's dinner on his head. He leaped to his feet, throwing cash down on the counter. "You stupid . . ."

Sputtering and blinking, Bart reached over the counter and grabbed a rag to mop himself off. He found chunks of beef stuck in his hair, and popped them into his mouth, chewing tentatively.

Waitress Annie waddled up, her mouth a cavernous O. Before she could speak, Bart and Rocco ran out of the restaurant and circled around to the back. But there were only vehicles in the parking lot, no Homer. They inspected the open air vent on the side of the building.

"He's got to be here somewhere," declared Rocco. "You take the bushes, I'll check the road."

A man exited the restaurant, climbed into his car, and started it up. A filthy Homer rolled out from underneath and banged on the driver's window. But the man jumped at the sight of the boy's soot-blackened face and peeled out, sending him flying.

Spotting Bart, Homer dived behind a truck. He heard a car pull up, doors slam, then muffled voices and foot-steps. Suddenly a hand clamped over his mouth.

Homer was dragged out of hiding. He bit the hand and ran.

"Oowwww!" Bart danced in agony, clutching his hand.

Homer ducked behind a car and edged along its sides, testing the doors—all locked. As he slid past the trunk, he brushed against its lock, and it popped. Slip-ping inside the trunk, he gently pulled it shut.

*End of ***Saving Bluestone Belle*** book excerpt*

Did You Enjoy This Book?

Dear Kind Reader,

If you enjoyed **The Cloud Horse & Other Stories** *and would like to help me reach more parents and kids with this book, please take a moment to write a brief review on Amazon. Your review makes a real difference, and I'd appreciate it very much.*

Thanks in advance!

With love,

Strawberry Shakespeare

About the Author

Strawberry Shakespeare was born and educated in New York City where she received a master's degree and doctoral training in clinical psychology. While working in the mental health field, she returned to her original love - writing - and is now a bestselling children's author and screenwriter.

Saving Bluestone Belle, Shakespeare's debut novel, is a popular children's book for ages 8-12, and has been a book club selection, a featured attraction and an award winner at book groups, book fairs, book festivals and animal rights conferences across the country. Her other bestselling children's books include ***The Cloud Horse & Other Stories*** and ***Hope's Horse: The Mystery of Shadow Ridge.***

Shakespeare was interviewed by reporters at the Animal Rights National Conference in Los Angeles. What follows is a quote from that interview.

"How we treat the least among us is an indication of who we really are as a culture. Too often, horses are viewed as a

disposable commodity rather than as faithful companions and helpmates of man. I was horrified by reports of their rampant abuse and exploitation by the horse slaughter industry, and decided to highlight this issue in my children's books. My hope is that this story will inspire young people to take a stand against cruelty toward horses and other animals."

Please read on to discover more books by Strawberry Shakespeare that your child is sure to love.

Children's Books by Strawberry Shakespeare

Saving Bluestone Belle

If your horse-loving kid enjoyed ***The Cloud Horse & Other Stories,*** you can be certain they will absolutely adore ***Saving Bluestone Belle*** by bestselling children's author Strawberry Shakespeare. This teacher-approved, award-winning comic-adventure is guaranteed to make your child laugh out loud and keep turning the pages with breathless excitement.

Saving Bluestone Belle tells about a stolen white horse and the ten-year-old boy who hits the road to rescue her. Along the way, young Homer goes up against an evil rancher and his wacky henchmen, only to be held captive in an underground fortress where he must use his quirky ingenuity to escape before it is too late!

This Disney-style story has been a featured attraction at children's book clubs, book fairs, book festivals and animal rights conferences across the country. It teaches children to be true to themselves and to care for the vulnerable creatures among us. Both avid and reluctant readers, boys and girls alike, will love the emphasis on snappy dialogue and fast-moving, action-oriented narrative.

The second edition of this popular book has been updated and enhanced by a new cover and additional interior illustrations, bringing the total number of original works by the talented contemporary artist, Mike Bilz, to 12. With its rollicking tale and delightful art, ***Saving Bluestone Belle*** is certain to thoroughly entertain the horse kids among you as well as the entire family.

Saving Bluestone Belle is a 174 page novel for ages 8-12. The new second edition is available on Amazon in two formats: Kindle and paperback. The first edition hardcover collectible is also available on Amazon.

Hope's Horse
The Mystery of Shadow Ridge

In this exciting novel by Strawberry Shakespeare, a 12-year-old girl, accompanied by the wild mustang she calls a friend, is drawn into a decades-old mystery surrounding the scary 'man on the mountain' and a strange metallic object buried in the woods.

Hope's Horse: The Mystery of Shadow Ridge, by best-selling children's author Strawberry Shakespeare, is a riveting mystery-adventure tale for young readers ages 9-12. Set in the California Eastern Sierras, it tells the story of twelve-year-old Hope Miller and her wild mustang, Tango.

While recovering from the death of her beloved grandfather, who shared her love of horses, Hope is forbidden by her parents to go on the mountain alone or anywhere near the wild horses she adores. So the girl keeps her horse, Tango, a secret from her parents, and rides him on the mountain without their knowledge.

On one of these outings, she and Tango evade evil poachers only to encounter a scary old mountain man. Escaping in a mad dash up the dark side of the mountain, they discover a mysterious metal object buried on Shadow Ridge. Hope instinctively knows her find is important and that she should tell her parents about it. But if she tells, she would also have to reveal the truth about her and Tango, and would probably never see him again.

A surprising turn of events merges the destinies of Hope, Tango and the old man on the mountain during a life-threatening confrontation with dangerous horse poachers. The resulting explosion of action, excitement, heartbreak and, ultimately, joyous healing is a must-read experience for the whole family and for every kid who loves adventure and horse stories.

Hope's Horse: The Mystery of Shadow Ridge is available on Amazon in print and Kindle editions. It is also available at BarnesandNoble.com.

The Cloud Horse & Other Stories

Your horse kids ages 8-12 will also love ***The Cloud Horse & Other Stories*** by Strawberry Shakespeare. This delightful volume contains unforgettable and uplifting horse stories for children.

Boys and girls who can't get enough of horses and adventure will adore the title story, "The Cloud Horse," an exhilarating yarn about a kid who is whisked away on the back of a flying horse!

Based on "The Boy Who Rode into the Sunset," by Australian author C. J. Dennis, this classic tale is a personal favorite of children's author Strawberry

Shakespeare. In her quest to bring it to modern audiences, she made several valuable enhancements to the original. These include creating an evocative new story title, designing a beautiful book cover, adapting the story as a novelette with eight exciting chapters, and penning a fascinating chapter on the life and times of C. J. Dennis, all of which render this magical fable more meaningful and enjoyable than ever.

This volume also contains three extraordinary short stories by bestselling children's author Strawberry Shakespeare. Readers of all ages will be enchanted by these mystical and inspiring tales.

The ebook and paperback editions of The ***Cloud Horse & Other Stories*** are available on Amazon.com.

All of the children's horse books by Strawberry Shakespeare make perfect gifts for young readers. Order them now. Kids treasure these bestselling tales and so will you!

Free Gift

The Reading Advantage

Quick & Easy Ways to Transform Your Child into a Passionate Reader!

As my thanks to all the wonderful parents, grandparents and teachers who have read ***The Cloud Horse & Other Stories,*** I would like you to have the bonus ebook, ***The Reading Advantage: Quick & Easy Ways to Transform Your Child into a Passionate Reader***. Written by psychologist/author Strawberry Shakespeare, this ebook provides powerful techniques that will not only increase your child's interest in reading but will also bring you and your child closer.

The research proves that avid readers have an advantage in life. Now you can give your child the same reading advantage. Visit https://bit.ly/TheReadingAdvantage/ to download your free gift.

Made in the USA
Columbia, SC
28 November 2020

25783423R00063